## Dear Parent:
## Your child's love of reading starts here!

Every child learns to read in a different way and at his or her own speed. Some go back and forth between reading levels and read favorite books again and again. Others read through each level in order. You can help your young reader improve and become more confident by encouraging his or her own interests and abilities. From books your child reads with you to the first books he or she reads alone, there are I Can Read Books for every stage of reading:

### SHARED READING
Basic language, word repetition, and whimsical illustrations, ideal for sharing with your emergent reader

### BEGINNING READING
Short sentences, familiar words, and simple concepts for children eager to read on their own

### READING WITH HELP
Engaging stories, longer sentences, and language play for developing readers

### READING ALONE
Complex plots, challenging vocabulary, and high-interest topics for the independent reader

### ADVANCED READING
Short paragraphs, chapters, and exciting themes for the perfect bridge to chapter books

**I Can Read Books** have introduced children to the joy of reading since 1957. Featuring award-winning authors and illustrators and a fabulous cast of beloved characters, I Can Read Books set the standard for beginning readers.

A lifetime of discovery begins with the magical words **"I Can Read!"**

*Visit www.icanread.com for information*
*on enriching your child's reading experience.*

 birds

 books

 card

 clock

 cookies

 door

 eyes

 flowers

 hot chocolate

 house

 mailbox

 pajamas

 ponies

 pony

 ribbons

 shoes

 sun

 tutu

# I Can Read!

BEGINNING
1
READING

# my little Pony™

# Sleepover Surprise

by Ruth Benjamin
illustrated by Josie Yee and Carlo LoRaso

HarperCollinsPublishers

Inside every  in

Ponyville was a

from Cherry Blossom.

She was having a

 party!

All of the

were invited.

The invite read:

*Please come to my* 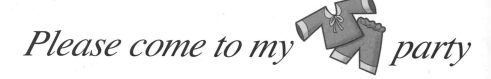 *party*

*tonight at midnight!*

*We will have*  *and* .

*Bring your favorite*

 *to share.*

*Be sure to take a nap*

*so you are not too sleepy!*

*Love, Cherry Blossom*

Petal Blossom was

the first  to get ready.

She loved parties!

She put  in her hair.

She put on her [image] .

She took a nap.

Triple Treat made

for the party.

She put on her  .

She took a nap.

Star Swirl picked
to bring to the party.
She tied the
with  .
She put on her  .
She took a nap.

Skywishes wished

she could take a nap.

But she was not tired.

She put on her dance

 and her  .

She danced until

the  went down.

Back at home, Skywishes

put on her .

"I am sleepy from dancing

so much," she said.

She looked at the .

"It is almost time

for the party.

I will close my

for just a minute."

At midnight,

the  went

to Cherry Blossom's  .

They drank  .

They ate  .

They read  .

"Where is Skywishes?"

they wondered.

The next morning,

Skywishes woke up.

The  was shining.

The were singing.

She looked at the .

"Oh, no!" she cried.

"I missed the party!"

Skywishes heard a

knock at the  .

It was Cherry Blossom

and the other  .

"I am sorry I missed the party,"

Skywishes told them.

"We missed you!" said

the  .

"So we brought the party to you!"

"Skywishes smiled.

"You are the best friends

a  could ask for!"

she said.